DISCARDED

Comets, Asteroids, and Meteoroids

Carmel Reilly

Marshall Cavendish
Benchmark
New York

This edition first published in 2012 in the United States of America by
Marshall Cavendish Benchmark
An imprint of Marshall Cavendish Corporation

All rights reserved.

No part of this publication may be reproduced, stored in a retrieval system or transmitted, in any form or by any means, electronic, mechanical, photocopying, recording, or otherwise, without the prior permission of the copyright owner. Request for permission should be addressed to the Publisher, Marshall Cavendish Corporation, 99 White Plains Road, Tarrytown, NY 10591. Tel: (914) 332-8888, fax: (914) 332-1888.

Website: www.marshallcavendish.us

This publication represents the opinions and views of the author based on Carmel Reilly's personal experience, knowledge, and research. The information in this book serves as a general guide only. The author and publisher have used their best efforts in preparing this book and disclaim liability rising directly and indirectly from the use and application of this book.

Other Marshall Cavendish Offices: Marshall Cavendish International (Asia) Private Limited, 1 New Industrial Road, Singapore 536196 • Marshall Cavendish International (Thailand) Co Ltd. 253 Asoke, 12th Flr, Sukhumvit 21 Road, Klongtoey Nua, Wattana, Bangkok 10110, Thailand • Marshall Cavendish (Malaysia) Sdn Bhd, Times Subang, Lot 46, Subang Hi-Tech Industrial Park, Batu Tiga, 40000 Shah Alam, Selangor Darul Ehsan, Malaysia

Marshall Cavendish is a trademark of Times Publishing Limited

All websites were available and accurate when this book was sent to press.

Library of Congress Cataloging-in-Publication Data

Reilly, Carmel, 1957-
  Asteroids, comets, and meteoroids / Carmel Reilly.
    p. cm. — (Sky watching)
  Includes index.
  Summary: "Provides scientific information about asteroids, comets, and meteoroids"—Provided by publisher.
  ISBN 978-1-60870-579-5
  1. Asteroids—Juvenile literature. 2. Comets—Juvenile literature. 3. Meteoroids—Juvenile literature. I. Title.
  QB651.R45 2012
  523.5—dc22
                                        2010044014

Publisher: Carmel Heron
Commissioning Editor: Niki Horin
Managing Editor: Vanessa Lanaway
Project Editor: Tim Clarke
Editor: Paige Amor
Proofreader: Helena Newton
Designer: Polar Design
Page layout: Romy Pearse
Photo Researcher: Legendimages
Illustrator: Adrian Hogan
Production Controller: Vanessa Johnson

Printed in China

Acknowledgments
The author and publisher are grateful to the following for permission to reproduce copyright material:

Front cover photograph: Comet Hale-Bopp among Andromeda courtesy of Photolibrary/Photo Researchers.

Photographs courtesy of: Dreamstime.com/Actionsports, **25**, /Njnightsky, **14** (right and bottom left), /Tmls, **23**; ESA/MPAe, Lindau, **12**; Getty Images/Jamie Cooper/SSPL, **8**; iStockphoto/Mike Sonnenberg, **5** (bottom), /Sergii Tsololo, border element throughout; NASA/JPL-Caltech, **11**, /JPL-Caltech/UCLA, **29**, /Lunar and Planetary Laboratory, **5** (top); Photolibrary/Photo Researchers, **1**, **14** (top left), /Science Photo Library/Jonathan Burnett, **28**, /Science Photo Library/Mark Garlick, **19**, /Science Photo Library/Walter Astropics, **9**, /Detlev van Ravenswaay, **15**.

While every care has been taken to trace and acknowledge copyright, the publisher tenders their apologies for any accidental infringement where copyright has proved untraceable. They would be pleased to come to a suitable arrangement with the rightful owner in each case.

Please Note
At the time of printing, the Internet addresses appearing in this book were correct. Owing to the dynamic nature of the Internet, however, we cannot guarantee that all these addresses will remain correct.

Contents

Sky Watching	4
Comets, Asteroids, and Meteoroids	5
What Are Space Rocks?	6
What Do Space Rocks Look Like from Earth?	8
What Are Space Rocks Made of?	10
Where Do We Find Space Rocks?	16
How Do Space Rocks Affect Earth?	24
What Does the Future Have in Store for Space Rocks?	26
What Is the Best Way to Watch Space Rocks?	30
Glossary	31
Index	32

Glossary Words
Words that are printed in **bold** are explained in the glossary on page 31.

What Does It Mean?
Words that are within a **box** are explained in the "What Does It Mean?" panel at the bottom of the page.

Sky Watching

When we sky watch, we look at everything above Earth. This includes both the material in Earth's **atmosphere** and the objects we can see beyond it, in space.

Why Do We Sky Watch?

Sky watching helps us to understand more about Earth's place in space. Earth is our home. It is also a planet that is part of a space neighborhood called the **solar system**. When we sky watch we learn about Earth, and our neighbors inside and outside the solar system.

What Objects Are in the Sky?

There are thousands of objects in the sky above Earth. These are Earth's neighbors—the Sun, the Moon, planets, stars, and flying space rocks (**comets**, **asteroids**, and **meteoroids**). Some can be seen at night and others can be seen during the day. Although some are visible with the human eye, all objects must be viewed through a **telescope** to be seen more clearly.

When and How Can We See Objects in the Sky?

Object in the Sky	Visible with Only the Human Eye	Visible Only through a Telescope	Visible during the Day	Visible at Night
Earth's Atmosphere	✗	✗	✗	✗
Sun	✓ (Do not view directly)	✗ (View only with a special telescope)	✓	✗
Moon	✓	✗	Sometimes	✓
Planets	Sometimes	Sometimes	Sometimes	✓
Stars	Sometimes	Sometimes	✗	✓
Comets	Sometimes	Sometimes	✗	✓
Asteroids	Sometimes	Sometimes	✗	✓
Meteoroids	Sometimes	Sometimes	✗	✓

WHAT DOES IT MEAN?

space The area in which the solar system, stars, and galaxies exist, also known as the universe.

Comets, Asteroids, and Meteoroids

Comets, asteroids, and meteoroids are small space objects. They are often called space rocks. Sometimes these objects are visible at night with the human eye, or through a telescope. At other times they cannot be seen from Earth at all.

Space-Rock Watching

People have always watched comets, asteroids, and meteoroids. When telescopes were invented 500 years ago, **astronomers** were able to study them closely. Now, thanks to space exploration, we have even more information about these objects. Today we know where space rocks come from, what they are made of, and how they can affect Earth.

Sky watching can be done during the day or night, with or without a telescope. Just look up!

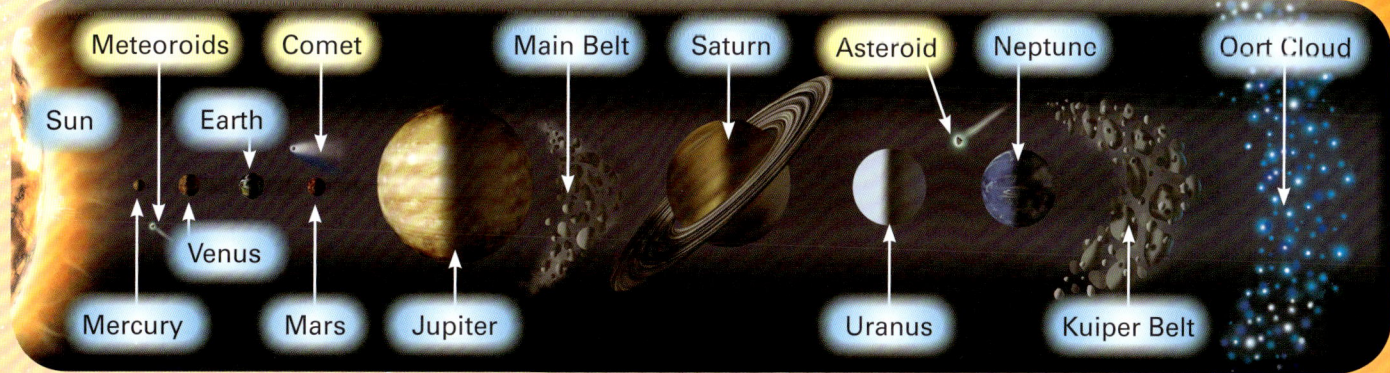

Comets, asteroids, and meteoroids can be found in many parts of our solar system. This diagram shows the approximate relative sizes of the Sun and the planets. The distances between them are not to scale.

WHAT DOES IT MEAN?

meteoroids Small space objects that are made of rock and metal, ranging from several feet wide to the size of a pea.

WHAT ARE SPACE ROCKS?

Comets, asteroids, and meteoroids are small space objects that were formed billions of years ago. They can be made up of different mixes of rock, ice, and metal. These space rocks are all moving through space, in [orbit] around the Sun and sometimes around other planets.

What are Comets, Asteroids, and Meteoroids?

Comets — Comets are made of rock and ice. The ice melts as they come near the Sun, and that causes their tails to form.

Asteroids — Asteroids are made mostly of rock. Most asteroids are solid but some are made of bits of rocks and dust.

Meteoroids — Meteoroids are made of rock and metal. They are small space objects that have broken, or been smashed, off asteroids and comets.

Space Rocks Formed from Leftover Gas and Dust

Comets, asteroids, and meteoroids were created when our solar system formed about 4.7 billion years ago. First, the Sun was born from a spinning cloud of **gas** and dust. Next, other **matter** orbiting around the Sun formed into planets. All of the leftover material became comets, asteroids, and meteoroids.

V Scientists are interested in studying space rocks because they are some of the oldest material in the solar system.

1. A cloud of dust and gas forms in space.
2. The cloud begins to spin and grow hot.
3. A ball of hot gases forms in the center and becomes our Sun.
4. Planets form from the dust and gas that spin around the Sun.
5. Leftover gas, dust, and rocks stick together and become comets, asteroids, and meteoroids.

WHAT DOES IT MEAN   **orbit** The path taken by one object that travels around another, larger one.

Space Rocks Are on the Move

Comets, asteroids, and meteoroids orbit the Sun. They are also often found in orbit around planets. The **gravity** of these larger space objects pulls comets, asteroids, and meteoroids as they move through space. The **gravitational pull** of the Sun and the planets keeps the space rocks on the same orbital path and stops them from flying off into space.

Space Rock Fact

Comets, asteroids, and meteoroids are too small to be planets. Asteroids and comets range in width from hundreds of miles to several feet. Meteoroids can be several feet wide, or the size of a pea.

Comets Can Change Their Orbits

Most comets orbit the Sun around the edge of our solar system. Over time, a few comets have changed their orbits and now swoop close to the Sun.

Asteroids Orbit in Groups and Alone

Most asteroids can be found orbiting in large groups in the **Main Belt** or at the edge of the solar system. Some asteroids orbit alone. This is often because they are caught in the gravity of a nearby planet and are pulled into orbit around it.

Meteoroids Orbit the Sun and Planets

Meteoroids orbit the Sun. They can also be found in orbit around all large objects in the solar system.

Main Belt—asteroids and meteoroids come from here

Kuiper Belt—asteroids, meteoroids, and some comets come from here

Hale Bopp (comet)

Eros (asteroid)

Amors (asteroids)

Halley's Comet

Oort Cloud—asteroids, meteoroids, and some comets come from here

 Comets, asteroids, and meteoroids move around different parts of the solar system.

What Do Space Rocks Look Like from Earth?

Most asteroids cannot be seen from Earth without a telescope. Comets and meteoroids can sometimes be seen from Earth with the human eye.

Asteroids Look Like Shining Stars

Most asteroids can only be seen through a telescope. They look like small dots of light. Asteroids seem to shine because their surfaces reflect the light of the Sun.

Comets Have Long, Glowing Tails

Some comets can be seen every few years as they pass Earth on their long orbit around the Sun. A comet looks like a fiery ball with a long, glowing tail in the night sky.

A comet can only be seen for a few nights from Earth as it orbits the Sun.

Famous Sky Watchers

In 1786, German-British astronomer Caroline Herschel, the sister of astronomer William Herschel, became the first woman to discover a comet. She went on to discover seven more comets, as well as many other space objects.

Meteoroids Look Like Shooting Stars

Meteoroids can only be seen from Earth when they enter the Earth's atmosphere and start to burn up. They are then called **meteors**. They are also sometimes called "shooting stars" because they look like flashes of starlight shooting across the sky. The bigger the meteoroid, the brighter the meteor. The brightest meteors are called fireballs.

Meteor Showers Look Like Fiery Rain

Meteor showers look like fiery rain falling from the sky. They are caused when a **meteoroid stream** passes through the Earth's atmosphere.

> ▼ Meteors can be seen somewhere in the sky almost every night. This huge meteor was seen falling to Earth during a meteor shower over the Mojave Desert in California.

Space Rock Fact

Meteoroids are rocks that travel through space. They are known as meteors when they enter the Earth's atmosphere and burn up. **Meteorites** are meteoroids that have reached Earth without burning up completely.

What Are Space Rocks Made Of?

From Earth, we cannot tell what is inside comets, asteroids, or meteoroids. Through space exploration, scientists have learned many things about these space rocks. Spacecraft send information to Earth, which is how scientists learn what these space objects are made of and what their surfaces are like.

Asteroids Are Mostly Made of Rock

Most asteroids are made of rock. Some are made from metal and have a heavy iron core. A very small number are made of half metal and half rock. Scientists believe that most asteroids are solid. Others are made of bits of rocks and dust that are stuck together by gravity.

Some asteroids are solid rock or metal, but others are made of rock and gravel.

Asteroids Are Covered in Regolith

Asteroids are covered in a layer of fine rock and dust called **regolith**. Larger asteroids are round, while smaller asteroids are irregular in shape. All asteroids have craters, or deep holes, that are caused by space object impacts.

Space Rock Fact

Asteroids can be large or tiny, but most are less than 328 feet (100 meters) wide. The largest asteroid is Ceres, which is almost 621 miles (1,000 kilometers) wide. Because it is so large and round, some scientists say that it is really a **dwarf planet**.

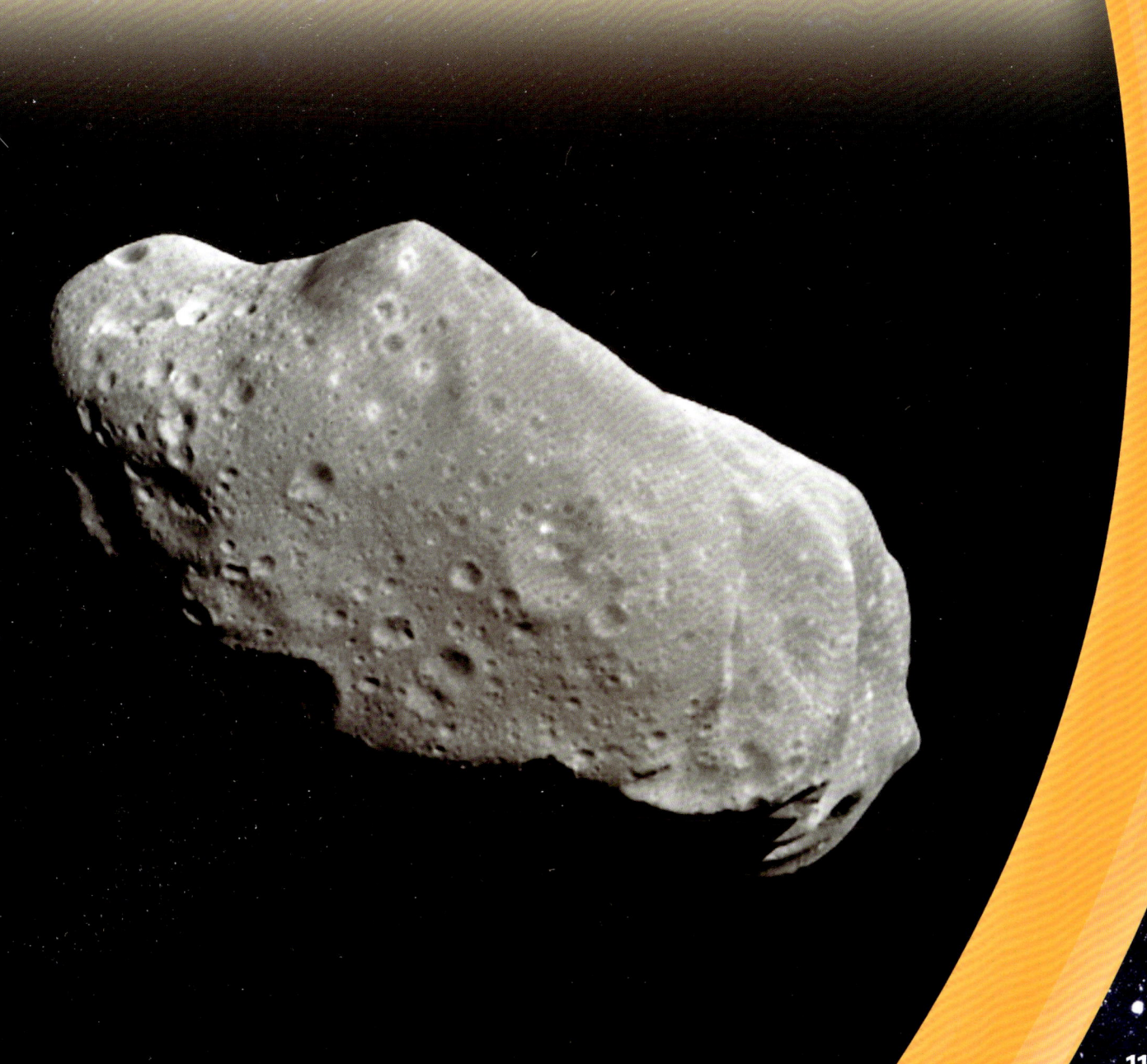

▼ This asteroid is called 243 Ida and is located in the Main Belt. It is covered in craters and has a thick layer of regolith.

Comets Are Made of Ice and Rock

The nucleus of a comet consists of a mix of ice and rock dust. This is why comets are sometimes called dirty snowballs. The ice is mostly water, with a small amount of frozen gases. The ice and dust mix is covered in a thin layer of dark dust.

Space Rock Fact

In 1986, a space probe called *Giotto* followed Halley's Comet as it orbited close to the Sun. The pictures *Giotto* sent back to Earth gave people the chance to see a comet up close for the first time.

∧ This photo of Halley's Comet was taken by the space probe *Giotto*.

WHAT DOES IT MEAN? **nucleus** The core or center of an object.

The Surface of Comets Changes

When a comet is far away from the Sun, it has a cold, dusty surface. When it comes closer to the Sun, it heats up and releases gas and dust. This forms a glowing cloud, called a coma, around the comet. It also forms two or three tails behind it.

The Size of Comets Changes

Most comets have a very small nucleus that is only a few miles wide when they are cold. When the comets heat up, their comas can be as wide as 62,137 mi. (100,000 km). Their tails can stretch as far as 62,137,120 mi. (100,000,000 km).

▼ Comets only have comas and tails when they are orbiting close to the Sun.

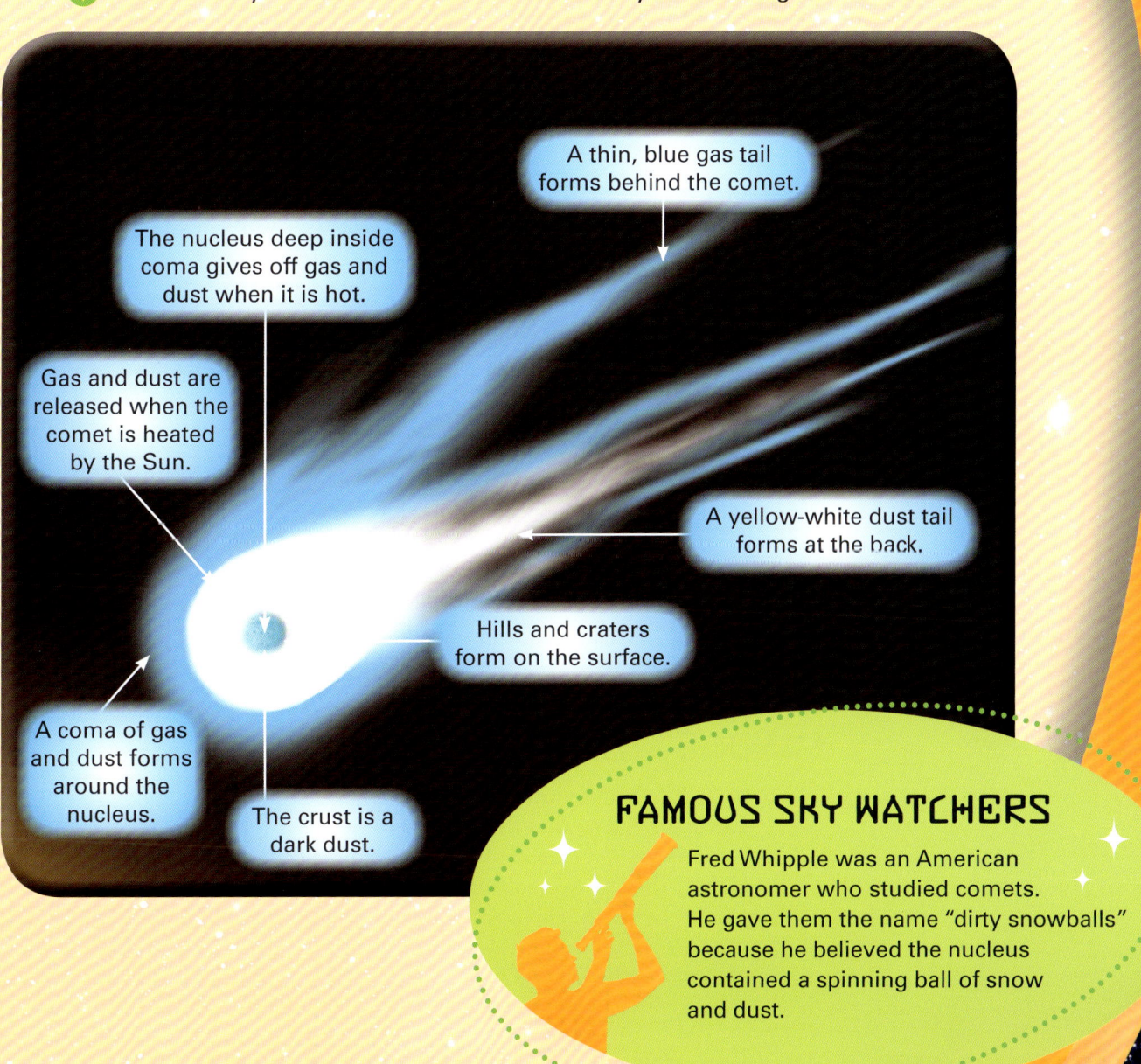

- A thin, blue gas tail forms behind the comet.
- The nucleus deep inside coma gives off gas and dust when it is hot.
- Gas and dust are released when the comet is heated by the Sun.
- A yellow-white dust tail forms at the back.
- Hills and craters form on the surface.
- A coma of gas and dust forms around the nucleus.
- The crust is a dark dust.

FAMOUS SKY WATCHERS

Fred Whipple was an American astronomer who studied comets. He gave them the name "dirty snowballs" because he believed the nucleus contained a spinning ball of snow and dust.

Meteoroids Are Made of Rock and Metal

Meteoroids are completely solid. There are three main kinds of meteoroids. Stony meteoroids are made of rock. Iron meteoroids are made of metal. Stony-iron meteoroids are made of both rock and metal.

Meteoroids Come in Many Sizes

Meteoroids range in size. Some are as big as very large boulders, while most are the size of pebbles, or even as small as a grain of sand.

▼ Most meteoroids are made of rock, some are made of metal, and a very few are made of rock and metal.

FAMOUS SKY WATCHERS

In 1866, Italian astronomer Giovanni Schiaparelli saw that the orbit of meteoroid streams he had observed were similar to the orbits of two comets that had also passed by Earth. He realized that these meteoroids were pieces that had broken off of comets.

Meteoroids Look Rough and Jagged

The surfaces of meteoroids look rough and jagged. This is because meteoroids are small pieces that have broken away or been smashed off of comets and asteroids.

Meteors Look Like They Are on Fire

From the outside, meteors look like they are on fire. As they enter Earth's atmosphere, friction makes the meteors so hot that they glow and their outside layers melt.

The Surfaces of Meteorites Are Melted

The surfaces of some meteorites are very smooth. Others have rough or bumpy surfaces. They vary depending on what the meteorites are made of and how much they melted as they entered Earth's atmosphere.

Space Rock Fact

When meteoroids enter Earth's atmosphere, the force of friction causes them to heat up. Many burn up completely but others slow down before reaching Earth's surface. In this way, Earth's atmosphere protects the planet from being pelted by space objects.

The surface of this iron meteorite was melted by the heat caused by friction as it traveled through Earth's atmosphere.

WHAT DOES IT MEAN **friction** A force that is created when one surface or object rubs against another, creating resistance.

Where Do We Find Space Rocks?

Comets, asteroids, and meteoroids all move through space in orbit around the Sun and the planets. Asteroids can be found in the Main Belt, in groups orbiting near planets and in the Kuiper Belt. Comets can be found around the Kuiper Belt and the Oort Cloud. Large numbers of meteoroids are found in all of these places.

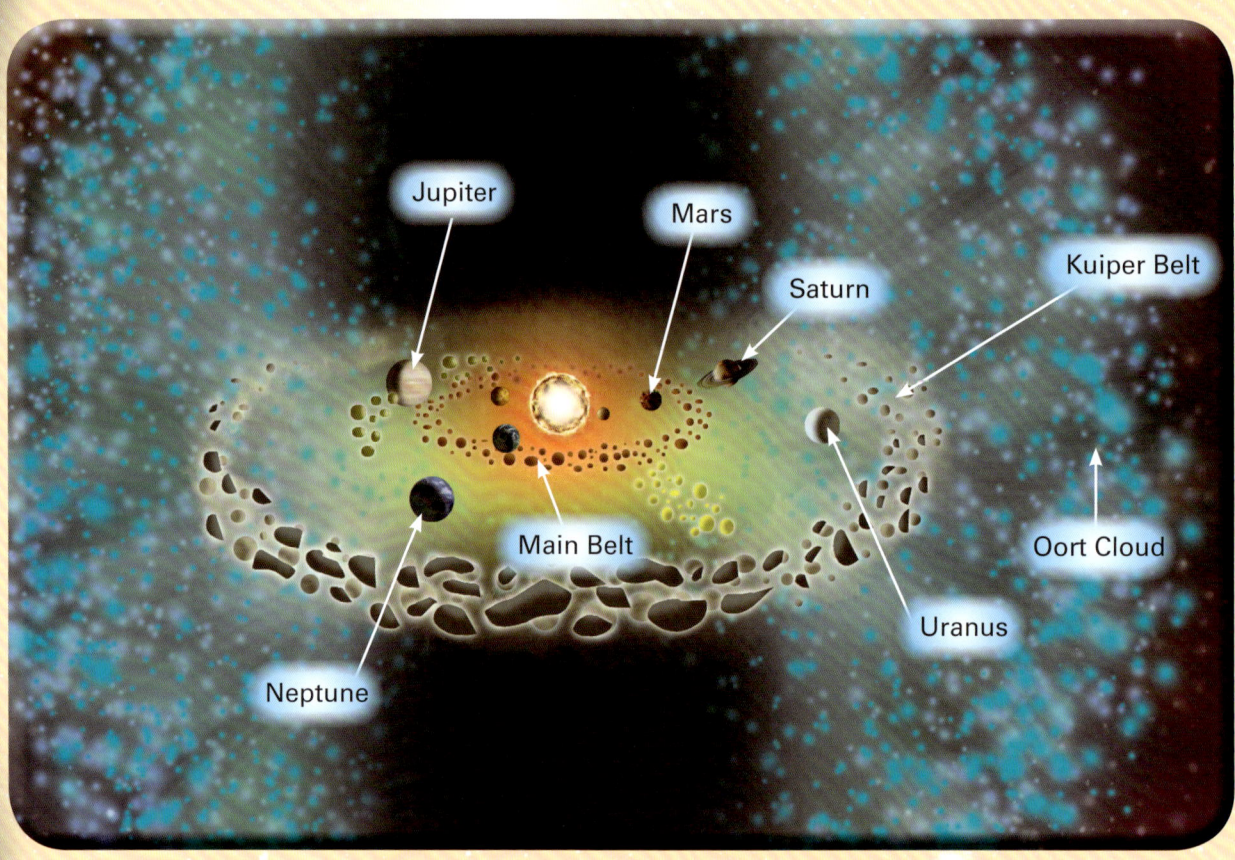

These are some of the places that space rocks can be found in the solar system.

Asteroids and Meteoroids Are Found in the Main Belt

The Main Belt, or the Asteroid Belt, lies halfway between Mars and Jupiter. It is about 248,550 mi. (400,000 km) from the Sun. Billions of small space objects, including meteoroids, also orbit the Sun in this area. Scientists believe these objects are leftover rubble from a planet that failed to form.

Most Asteroids Are in the Main Belt

The Main Belt contains 90 percent of all asteroids found in the solar system. These asteroids take between three and six years to complete their orbit around the Sun. They orbit in the same direction as the planets and they spin as they move.

V About ten asteroids in the Main Belt are bigger than 155 mi. (250 km) wide. However, most are only a few feet wide.

Space Rock Fact

Scientists think there were only about 650 asteroids when the solar system first came into being. However, they crashed into each other so often that they broke into billions of smaller objects.

Asteroids and Meteoroids Orbit Near Planets

Smaller groups of asteroids are found outside the Main Belt. They orbit near different planets. Groups called the Apollos, Atens, and Amors orbit close to Earth. Others, such as the Trojans and Centaurs, lie farther away from the Sun. Meteoroids that formed from space rock collisions orbit alongside these asteroids.

Apollos, Atens, and Amors Orbit Near Earth

Apollos, Atens, and Amors are called Near Earth Objects. They are found in areas not far from Earth. Their orbit around the Sun can bring them very close to our planet. The Atens sit mainly within Earth's orbit. The Amors orbit between Earth and Mars. The Apollos orbit near Mars.

V There are five major groups of asteroids that can be found outside the Main Belt.

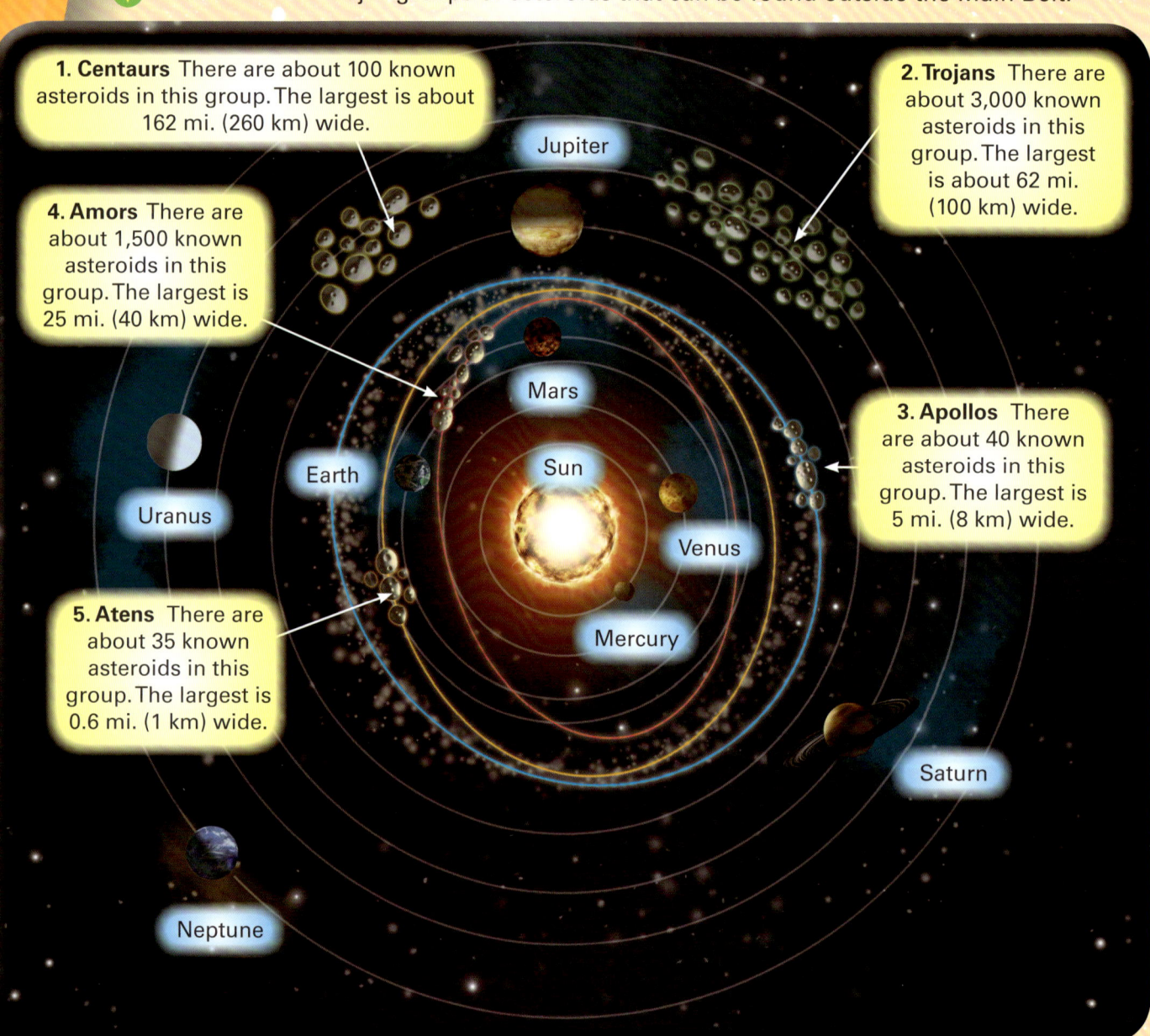

1. **Centaurs** There are about 100 known asteroids in this group. The largest is about 162 mi. (260 km) wide.

2. **Trojans** There are about 3,000 known asteroids in this group. The largest is about 62 mi. (100 km) wide.

3. **Apollos** There are about 40 known asteroids in this group. The largest is 5 mi. (8 km) wide.

4. **Amors** There are about 1,500 known asteroids in this group. The largest is 25 mi. (40 km) wide.

5. **Atens** There are about 35 known asteroids in this group. The largest is 0.6 mi. (1 km) wide.

Trojans Orbit with Jupiter

The Trojan group of asteroids lies beyond the Main Belt. They are in the same orbit as Jupiter. There are two groups of Trojans. One orbits in front of Jupiter and the other orbits behind it. There are thousands of asteroids in this group.

▼ Space probes have helped scientists discover thousands of Trojan asteroids in the past few years. This Trojan asteroid is known as 624 Hektor.

Centaurs Orbit with Saturn and Neptune

Centaur asteroids can be found at the edge of the solar system. They are rocky, icy objects that usually follow the same orbit as Saturn and Neptune. However, sometimes they behave like comets, following long, narrow orbits around the Sun. Meteoroids are also found in this area.

Space Rock Fact

In 1977 the first Centaur, Chiron, was found and classified as an asteroid. However, scientists noticed that as it orbited the Sun it seemed to behave more like a comet. Today it is classified as both an asteroid and a comet.

Comets and Meteoroids Are Found around the Kuiper Belt

The Kuiper Belt is a flat disc that is home to thousands of small space objects made of rock and ice, such as comets and meteoroids. It lies about 3.7 to 7.5 billion mi. (6–12 billion km) from the Sun. It is 20 times wider than the Main Belt.

The Kuiper Belt Is Beyond Neptune

The Kuiper Belt begins just past Neptune's orbit. Neptune is the most distant planet in our solar system. The Kuiper Belt was only discovered by astronomers in the 1990s. So far, astronomers have found more than a thousand objects there.

Astronomers think the Kuiper Belt might be home to more than 70,000 space objects, including comets and meteoroids.

FAMOUS SKY WATCHERS

The Kuiper Belt is named after Dutch-American astronomer Gerard Kuiper. In 1951, he created the theory that short-term comets come from a pool of rock and ice objects orbiting beyond Neptune. This was confirmed in the 1990s when the first object was discovered there.

The Kuiper Belt Has Short-Term Comets

Kuiper Belt objects are made up of rock, ice, and frozen gases. Some of these objects are known as short-term comets. Short-term comets take less than 200 years to orbit the Sun. They have long, oval-shaped orbits that take them close to the Sun and then back out to the Kuiper Belt.

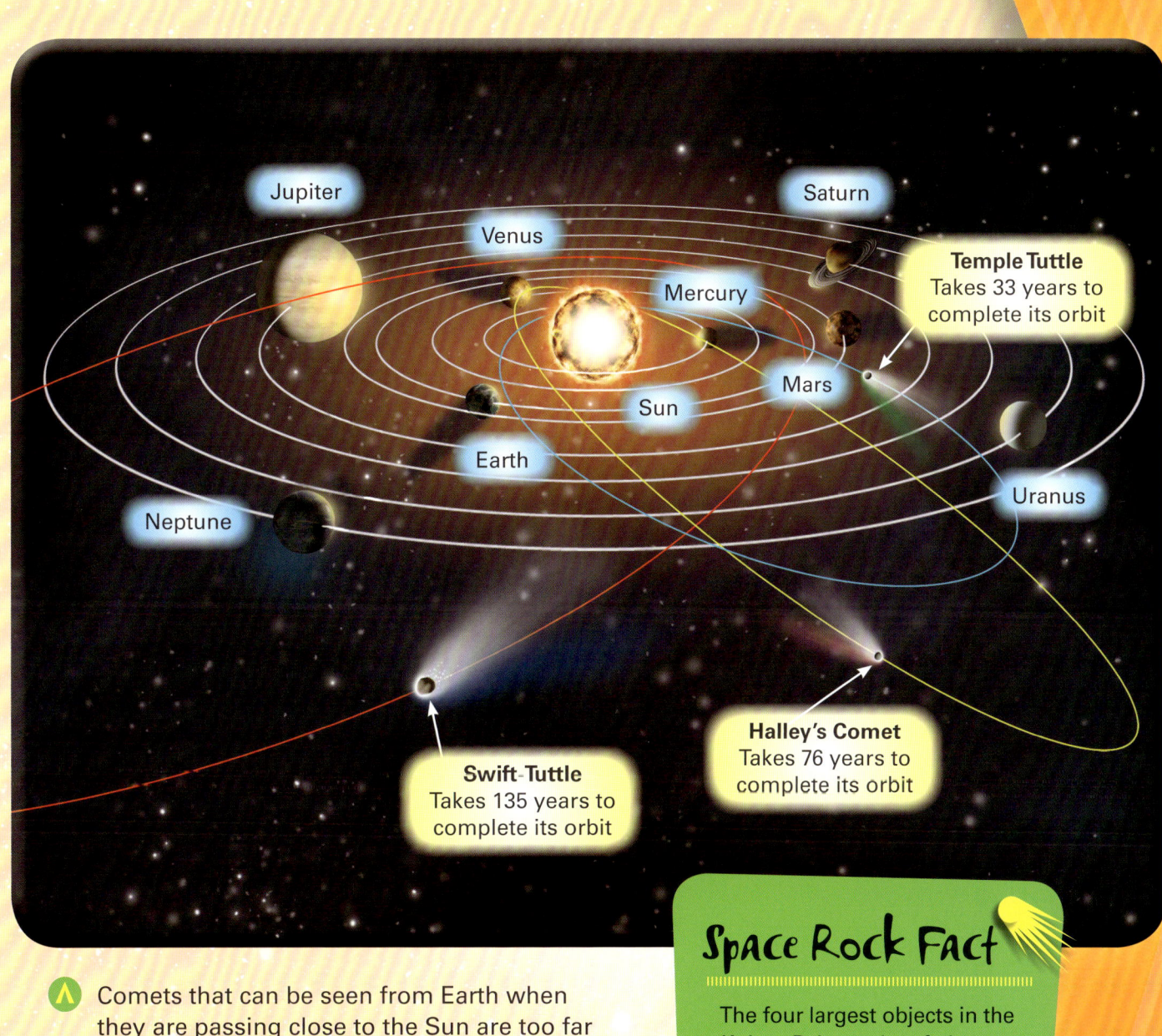

Comets that can be seen from Earth when they are passing close to the Sun are too far away to be seen at the other end of their orbit.

Space Rock Fact

The four largest objects in the Kuiper Belt are dwarf planets. They are called Eris, Pluto, Makemake, and Haumea. Dwarf planets are too small to be planets but too large to be asteroids or comets.

Comets and Meteoroids Are Found around the Oort Cloud

The Oort Cloud is a huge area at the very edge of our solar system. It is full of small, rocky, icy space objects, such as comets and meteoroids. The Oort Cloud lies about one light-year from the Sun. A light-year is the time it takes for light to travel in a year.

The Oort Cloud Is Made of Many Small Objects

There are billions of space objects in the Oort Cloud. If they were all put together, they would weigh about as much as three planet Earths.

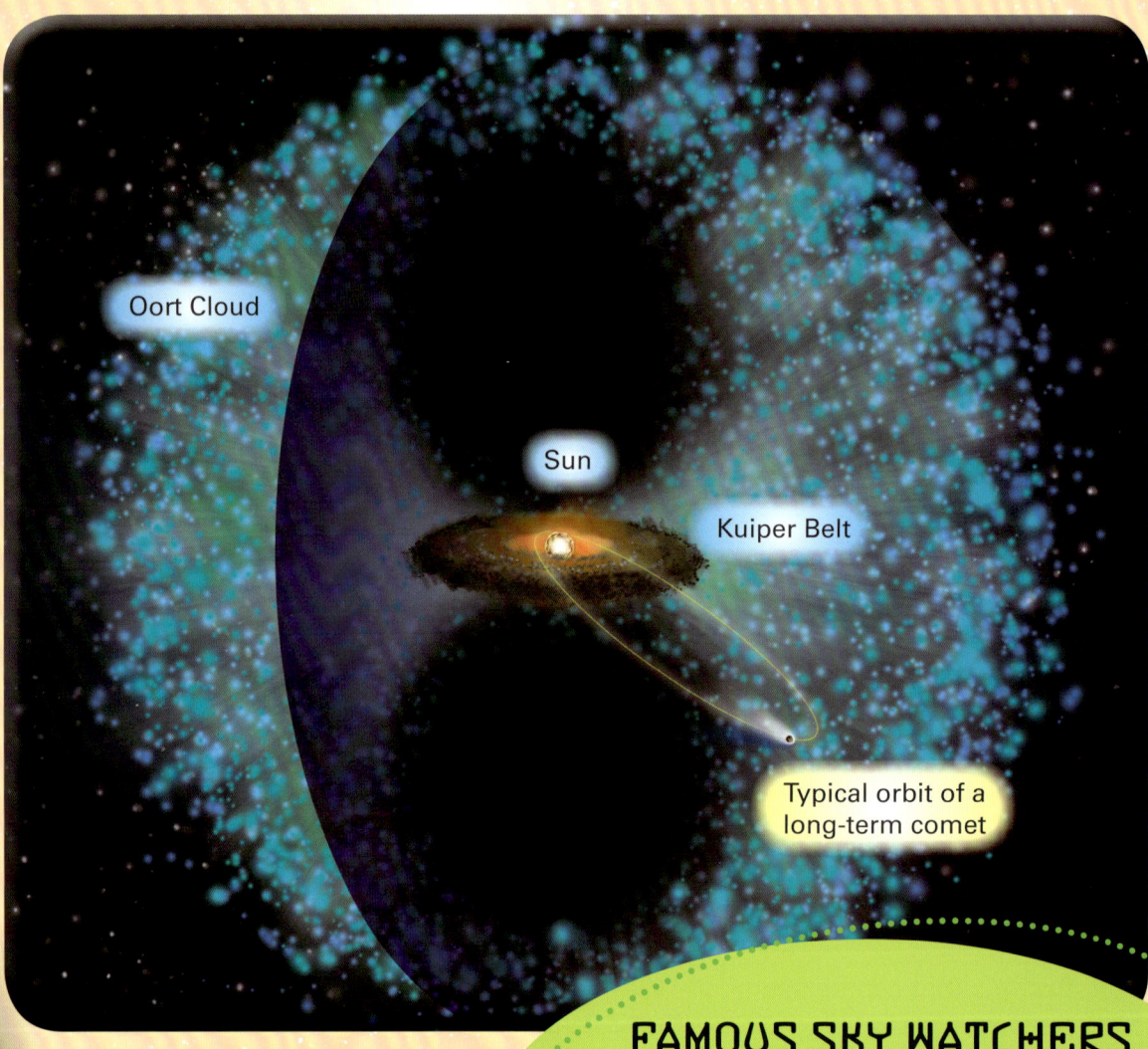

⚠ The Oort Cloud is made up of matter that was left over when the solar system was formed.

FAMOUS SKY WATCHERS

Jan Oort was a Dutch astronomer who believed that the solar system was surrounded by a huge cloud of long-term comets. When this cloud was discovered it was named after him.

The Oort Cloud Is at the Edge of Our Solar System

Comets at the very far edge of the Oort Cloud can take up to 10 million years to orbit the Sun. The pull of the Sun's gravity ends at the edge of the Oort Cloud. If a comet passes this point it will fly off into space.

The Oort Cloud Has Long-Term Comets

The Oort Cloud is home to many long-term comets. Long-term comets take more than 200 years to orbit the Sun. Many take thousands of years to complete their journeys. Because of this, people have observed very few long-term comets.

▽ Comet Hale-Bopp takes 4,200 years to orbit around the Sun and return to the Oort Cloud.

Space Rock Fact

Long-term comet Hale-Bopp was one of the brightest comets to have been viewed from Earth. It was first observed in 1995. It could be seen without a telescope for a record 18 months, from May 1996 until December 1997.

How Do Space Rocks Affect Earth?

Although we cannot always see them from Earth, comets, asteroids, and meteoroids can have huge effects on our planet. Comets and asteroids have smashed into Earth, causing much damage, and could do so again. Meteorites fall to Earth every day.

Asteroids and comets crash to Earth, creating impact craters.

There is danger on Earth from comet, asteroid, and meteroid impacts.

Comets, asteroids, and meteoroids affect Earth in a number of ways.

Comets and Asteroids Create Impact Craters on Earth

About 150 impact craters have been found on Earth. Impact craters are large holes caused by space object crashes. One of the largest is near the coast of Mexico and is 124 mi. (200 km) wide. It was made 65 million years ago by an asteroid or comet. Many scientists think the crash that made this crater also destroyed much of life on Earth at the time, including the dinosaurs.

Earth Is in Danger from Space Rock Impacts

Astronomers study the skies for any small space objects that are likely to strike Earth. Impacts from large meteorites or asteroids are more powerful than atomic bombs. They can cause earthquakes and tsunami waves. They can also throw dust into the atmosphere that will block the Sun for years. An impact like this could wipe out life on Earth.

▼ The Berringer Meteor Crater was made by a meteorite that fell to Earth thousands of years ago. It is the largest known impact crater on Earth. It is in Arizona.

Space Rock Fact

Although most meteoroids burn up in Earth's atmosphere, many reach the ground. It is thought that about 22 tons (20 tonnes) of space matter lands on Earth each year.

What Does the Future Have in Store for Space Rocks?

People have always wondered about what happens to the comets, asteroids, and meteors they see in the night sky. Will these objects always exist? Will they be dangerous to Earth? Astronomers are now able to answer some of these questions.

Asteroids Are Getting Smaller and Smaller

When the solar system was formed, asteroids were much bigger than they are now. Over time, they have crashed into each other and broken into smaller pieces. It is very likely that asteroids will keep breaking into smaller and smaller pieces.

▼ When asteroids crash they break down into smaller asteroids and meteoroids.

FAMOUS SKY WATCHERS

The National Aeronautics and Space Administration (NASA) is the U.S. government space agency. NASA has a Near Earth Object program, which searches for space objects that are likely to threaten Earth. These objects can then be redirected away from Earth, or destroyed.

Comets Are Breaking Up and Leaving the Solar System

Comets do not keep orbiting the Sun forever. Some melt away, while others are knocked out of their orbits and fly out of our solar system.

Comets Are Melting

Comets that orbit close to the Sun slowly break up. Each time they pass the Sun, the ice in their nucleus melts and they loose water and gas. Eventually, there is not enough ice left to hold the dust together and the comet breaks up.

Comets Are Knocked Out of Their Orbit

Comets can be knocked out of their orbits by other objects. This causes them to fly off into space. Comets at the very edge of the Oort Cloud can also be pulled away from the solar system by another star's gravity.

As a comet comes close to the Sun its ice melts and it loses water and gases.

After being heated many times by the Sun, there is not enough ice to hold the dust together.

Some comets will pass the Sun up to 100 times before they lose all their gas and dust.

Meteoroids Burn Up or Become Meteorites

Meteoroids are often caught in the gravity of larger space objects. This causes them to crash into the other object and break up. When meteoroids are pulled toward planets with a thick atmosphere, they usually burn up before they hit the planet itself. Those that do not burn up become a part of the surface of the planet.

⋀ Some meteors that burn up or explode in Earth's atmosphere are known as fireballs. They are brighter than most meteors and are even brighter than the planets in the sky.

Space Rock Fact

Many thousands of meteors burn up in Earth's atmosphere every year. About 5,000 of these break up and explode. Exploding meteors are called bolides.

New Space Rocks Will Be Created

When our solar system breaks apart, all the matter of which it was formed will be used again to create new planets and stars. New comets, asteroids, and meteoroids will be created from the leftover matter.

The End of Our Solar System

In about 5 billion years, our solar system will start to die. All of the planets and small space objects near the Sun will burn up. Later, as the Sun cools, the remaining planets and space objects will drift off into space.

The Beginning of a New Solar System

All of the matter that has been a part of our solar system will be used again. The gases and dust from comets, asteroids, meteoroids, and other space objects will form a nebula. From this nebula a new star or solar system will be born.

> New solar systems form in huge swirling clouds of gases and dust known as nebulas. Any leftover gas, dust, and rocks become new comets, asteroids, and meteoroids.

WHAT DOES IT MEAN?

nebula A cloud of gas and dust in space.

What Is the Best Way to Watch Space Rocks?

You can sometimes see comets and meteors in the sky with just the human eye. They can be seen more clearly through a telescope or **binoculars**. However, asteroids are hard to see, even with powerful telescopes.

Comet Watching

Every year, a number of comets pass close enough to Earth to be seen. To find how and when to view these comets, visit a nearby planetarium or observatory, or look at their website.

Asteroid Watching

The best way to view asteroids is to look at photos of them online. Visit the websites of space agencies such as NASA (www.nasa.gov) and the Japan Aerospace Exploration Agency (JAXA, www.jaxa.jp/index_e.html).

Meteor Watching

Although meteors can be seen at any time in the night, the best time to view them is early in the morning, around 4 a.m. Ask your parents to wake up early with you.

Useful Equipment for Backyard Astronomy	
Equipment	**What It Is Used for**
 Binoculars or a Telescope	A pair of binoculars or a telescope will help you see comets and meteors as they cross the sky.
 Sky Chart	A sky chart will help you to see any new objects in the sky.
 Compass	A compass will help you face the right direction when you are looking for comets.
Flashlight with Red Cellophane over the Lightbulb	Use a flashlight to help you read the sky chart. Putting red cellophane over the lightbulb end of the flashlight will prevent its light from affecting your night vision.

Useful Websites

Asteroids and Comets: http://science.nationalgeographic.com/science/space/solar-system/asteroids-comets-article/

Comet Hale-Bopp Images: http://www2.jpl.nasa.gov/comet/images.html

Space Station Meteor Shower: http://science.nasa.gov/science-news/science-at-nasa/2002/17may_issmeteors/

Glossary

asteroids	Small, rocky, or metal space objects that orbit the Sun.
astronomers	People who study stars, planets, and other bodies in space.
atmosphere	The layer of gases that surrounds a planet, moon, or star.
binoculars	An instrument with two eye pieces, for making faraway objects look bigger.
comets	Small, rocky, and icy space objects that have long, shining tails that appear when orbiting near the Sun.
dwarf planet	A space object that is not quite big enough to be a planet, but is too big to be an asteroid.
friction	The force that is created when one surface or object rubs against another, creating resistance.
gas	A substance that is not solid or liquid, and is usually invisible.
gravitational pull	The forces of gravity that attract two objects toward each other.
gravity	The force that attracts all objects toward each other.
impact craters	Large, round holes made by a small space object crashing into a larger one.
Main Belt	The region of the solar system where most asteroids are found.
matter	A substance of a particular kind, such as gas and dust.
meteorites	Meteoroids that reach Earth's surface without burning up completely.
meteoroids	Small space objects that are made of rock and metal, ranging from several feet wide to the size of a pea.
meteoroid stream	A trail of rocks and dust that follows a comet, forming the comet's tail.
meteors	Meteoroids that have entered Earth's atmosphere and burn up.
nebula	A cloud of gas and dust in space.
nucleus	The core or center of an object.
orbit	The path taken by a space object that travels around another, larger space object.
regolith	A layer of rock and dust found on space objects.
solar system	The Sun and everything that orbits it, including planets and other space objects.
space	The area in which the solar system, stars, and galaxies exist, also known as the universe.
telescope	An instrument with a single eye piece, for making faraway objects look bigger.

INDEX

A
Amors, 7, 16, 18
Apollos, 16, 18
Atens, 16, 18
atmosphere, 4, 9, 15, 25, 28

B
bolides, 28

C
Centaurs, 16, 18, 19
Ceres, 11
Chiron, 19
comas (of comets), 13
craters, 11, 24, 25

D
dwarf planets, 11, 21

E
Earth, 4, 5, 8, 9, 10, 12, 14, 15, 18, 21, 22, 23, 24–25, 26, 28, 30
Eris, 21

F
fireballs, 9, 28
friction, 15

G
gases, 6, 12, 13, 21, 27, 29
Giotto space probe, 12
gravity, 7, 10, 23, 27, 28

H
Hale-Bopp, 23, 30
Halley's Comet, 12, 21
Haumea, 21

J
Jupiter, 5, 16, 19, 21

K
Kuiper Belt, 5, 7, 16, 20–21, 22

M
Main Belt, 5, 7, 11, 16–17, 18, 19, 20
Makemake, 21
Mars, 5, 16, 18, 21
meteorites, 9, 15, 24, 25, 28
meteoroid streams, 9, 14
meteors, 9, 15, 25, 26, 28, 30
meteor showers, 9, 30

N
NASA (National Aeronautics and Space Administration), 26, 30
Near Earth Objects, 18, 26
nebulas, 29
Neptune, 5, 16, 19, 20, 21

O
Oort Cloud, 5, 7, 16, 22–23, 27
orbits (of space rocks), 6, 7, 8, 12, 13, 14, 16, 17, 18–19, 20, 21, 22, 23, 27

P
planets, 4, 5, 6, 7, 11, 15, 16, 17, 18–19, 20, 21, 22, 24, 28, 29
Pluto, 21

R
regolith, 11

S
624 Hektor, 19
Saturn, 5, 16, 19, 21
solar system, 4, 5, 6, 7, 16, 17, 19, 20, 22, 26, 27, 29
Sun, 4, 5, 6, 7, 8, 12, 13, 16, 17, 18, 19, 20, 21, 22, 23, 25, 27, 29
surfaces of space rocks, 8, 10, 13, 15

T
243 Ida, 11
tails (of comets), 6, 8, 13
Trojans, 16, 18, 19